The PELICAN CHORUS AND OTHER NONSENSE BY EDWARD LEAR ILLUSTRATED BY FRED MARCELLINO

A
atheneum

★ ATHENEUM BOOKS FOR YOUNG READERS ★ NEW YORK LONDON TORONTO SYDNEY NEW DELHI ★

For Angela, my mother
—F. M.

ATHENEUM BOOKS FOR YOUNG READERS
An imprint of Simon & Schuster Children's Publishing Division
1230 Avenue of the Americas, New York, New York 10020
ATHENEUM BOOKS FOR YOUNG READERS
is a registered trademark of Simon & Schuster, Inc.
Atheneum logo is a trademark of Simon & Schuster, Inc.
For information about special discounts for bulk purchases,
please contact Simon & Schuster Special Sales
at 1-866-506-1949 or business@simonandschuster.com.
The Simon & Schuster Speakers Bureau can bring authors to your live event.
For more information or to book an event, contact the Simon & Schuster Speakers Bureau
at 1-866-248-3049 or visit our website at www.simonspeakers.com.
Book design by Fred Marcellino
The text for this book was set in LTC Cloister.
The illustrations for this book were rendered in watercolor on Arches Aquarelle stock.
Manufactured in China
0817 SCP
First Atheneum Books for Young Readers edition October 2017
2 4 6 8 10 9 7 5 3 1
Library of Congress Cataloging-in-Publication Data
Names: Lear, Edward, 1812-1888. author. | Marcellino, Fred, illustrator.
Title: Pelican chorus / Edward Lear ; illustrated by Fred Marcellino.
Description: First edition. | New York : Atheneum Books for Young Readers, [2017]
Identifiers: LCCN 2016034571
ISBN 9781481470490 (hardcover)
ISBN 9781481470506 (eBook)
Subjects: LCSH: Nonsense verses, English. | Children's poetry, English.
Classification: LCC PR4879.L2 P43 2017 | DDC 821/.8—dc23
LC record available at https://lccn.loc.gov/2016034571

There lived an old man in the Kingdom of Tess,
Who invented a purely original dress;

And when it was perfectly made and complete,
He opened the door, and walked into the street.

By way of a hat, he'd a loaf of brown bread,
In the middle of which he inserted his head.
His shirt was made up of no end of dead mice,
The warmth of whose skins was quite fluffy and nice.
His drawers were of rabbit skins, so were his shoes;
His stockings were skins, but it is not known whose.
His waistcoat and trousers were made of pork chops;
His buttons were jujubes and chocolate drops.
His coat was all pancakes with jam for a border,
And a girdle of biscuits to keep it in order;
And he wore over all, as a screen from bad weather,
A cloak of green cabbage leaves stitched all together.

He had walked a short way when he heard a great noise,
Of all sorts of beasticles, birdlings, and boys;

And from every long street and dark lane in the town,
Beasts, birdles, and boys in a tumult rushed down.

Two cows and a half ate his cabbage-leaf cloak;

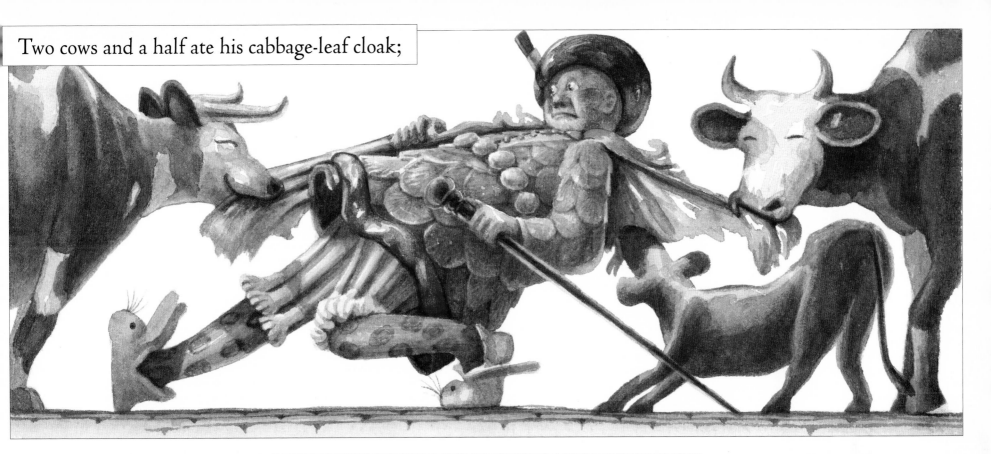

Four apes seized his girdle, which vanished like smoke.

Three kids ate up half of his pancaky coat,
And the tails were devour'd by an ancient he-goat.

An army of dogs in a twinkling tore *up* his
Pork waistcoat and trousers to give to their puppies.

And while they were growling, and mumbling the chops,
Ten boys prigged the jujubes and chocolate drops.

He tried to run back to his house, but in vain,
For scores of fat pigs came again and again;

They rushed out of stables and hovels and doors,
They tore off his stockings, his shoes, and his drawers.

And now from the housetops with screechings descend,
Striped, spotted, white, black, and gray cats without end.
They jumped on his shoulders and knocked off his hat;

When crows, ducks, and hens made a mincemeat of that,
They speedily flew at his sleeves in a trice,
And utterly tore up his shirt of dead mice.

They swallowed the last of his shirt with a squall,

Whereon he ran home with no clothes on at all.

And he said to himself as he bolted the door,
"I will not wear a similar dress any more,
Any more, any more, any more, never more!"

THE OWL AND THE PUSSYCAT

The Owl and the Pussycat went to sea
In a beautiful pea-green boat.

They took some honey, and plenty of money,
Wrapped up in a five-pound note.

The Owl looked up to the stars above,
And sang to a small guitar,
"O lovely Pussy! O Pussy, my love,
What a beautiful Pussy you are,
    You are
    You are!
What a beautiful Pussy you are!"

Pussy said to the Owl, "You elegant fowl!
How charmingly sweet you sing!

"O let us be married! too long we have tarried:
But what shall we do for a ring?"

They sailed away, for a year and a day,
To the land where the bong tree grows;

And there in a wood a Piggywig stood
With a ring at the end of his nose,
    His nose,
    His nose,
With a ring at the end of his nose.

"Dear Pig, are you willing to sell for one shilling
Your ring?" Said the Piggy, "I will."

So they took it away, and were married next day
By the Turkey who lives on the hill.

They dined on mince, and slices of quince,
Which they ate with a runcible spoon;

And hand in hand, on the edge of the sand,
They danced by the light of the moon,
    The moon,
    The moon,

They danced by the light of the moon.

King and Queen of the Pelicans we;
No other birds so grand we see!
None but we have feet like fins!
With lovely leathery throats and chins!

Ploffskin, Pluffskin, Pelican jee!
We think no birds so happy as we!
Plumpskin, Ploshkin, Pelican jill!
We think so then, and we thought so still!

We live on the Nile. The Nile we love.

By night we sleep on the cliffs above.

By day we fish, and at eve we stand

On long bare islands of yellow sand.

And when the sun sinks slowly down
And the great rock walls grow dark and brown,
Where the purple river rolls fast and dim
And the ivory ibis starlike skim,
Wing to wing we dance around,
Stamping our feet with a flumpy sound,
Opening our mouths as pelicans ought,
And this is the song we nightly snort:

Ploffskin, Pluffskin, Pelican jee,
We think no birds so happy as we!
Plumpskin, Ploshkin, Pelican jill,
We think so then, and we thought so still!

Last year came out our daughter, Dell;
And all the birds received her well.
To do her honor, a feast we made
For every bird that can swim or wade.

Herons and gulls, and cormorants black,
Cranes, and flamingos with scarlet back,
Plovers and storks, and geese in clouds,
Swans and dilberry ducks in crowds.

Thousands of birds in wondrous flight!
They ate and drank and danced all night,
And echoing back from the rocks you heard
Multitude-echoes from bird to bird.

Ploffskin, Pluffskin, Pelican jee,
We think no birds so happy as we!
Plumpskin, Ploshkin, Pelican jill,
We think so then, and we thought so still!

Yes, they came; and among the rest,
The King of the Cranes all grandly dressed.
Such a lovely tail! Its feathers float
Between the ends of his blue dress coat;

With pea-green trousers all so neat,
And a delicate frill to hide his feet.
(For though no one speaks of it, everyone knows,
He has got no webs between his toes!)

As soon as he saw our daughter, Dell,
In violent love that Crane King fell—
On seeing her waddling form so fair,
With a wreath of shrimps in her short white hair.

And before the end of the next long day,
Our Dell had given her heart away;

For the King of the Cranes had won that heart,
With a crocodile's egg and a large fish tart.

She vowed to marry the King of the Cranes,
Leaving the Nile for stranger plains;
And away they flew in a gathering crowd
Of endless birds in a lengthening cloud.

Ploffskin, Pluffskin, Pelican jee,
We think no birds so happy as we!
Plumpskin, Ploshkin, Pelican jill,
We think so then, and we thought so still!

And far away in the twilight sky,
We heard them singing a lessening cry,
Farther and farther till out of sight,
And we stood alone in the silent night!

Often since, in the nights of June,
We sit on the sand and watch the moon;
She has gone to the great Gromboolian plain,
And we probably never shall meet again!

Oft, in the long still nights of June,
We sit on the rocks and watch the moon;
She dwells by the streams of the Chankly Bore,
And we probably never shall see her more.

Ploffskin, Pluffskin, Pelican jee,

We think no birds so happy as we!

Plumpskin, Ploshkin, Pelican jill,

We think so then, and we thought so still!